# HATTER M
### THE
# NATURE
### OF
# WONDER
#### VOLUME THREE

To the Earth
and her infinite wonders...

# HATTER M
## THE
# NATURE OF WONDER
### VOLUME THREE

*Written by Frank Beddor & Liz Cavalier*

*Art by Sami Makkonen*

AUTOMATIC
PICTURES
PUBLISHING

# Hatter M: The Nature of Wonder
Volume 3

**Writers**
Frank Beddor
Liz Cavalier

**Art**
Sami Makkonen

**Cover Art**
Vance Kovacs

**Letterer**
Tom B. Long

**Editor**
C.J. Wrobel

**Reconnaissance & Analysis**
Nate Barlow

**White Flower Raconteur**
Miss Emily McGuiness

**Guest Writer/Researcher**
Christopher Monfette

**Logo Designed by**
Christina Craemer

**Interiors Designed by**
Vera Milosavich

**Institute Artists**
Brian Flora
Tae Young Choi
Catia Chien
Vance Kovacs

www.lookingglasswars.com

The Looking Glass Wars® is a trademark of Automatic Pictures, Inc.
Copyright © 2010 Automatic Pictures, Inc. All rights reserved.

"Prologue", from *ArchEnemy: The Looking Glass Wars*®, *Book Three* by Frank Beddor,
Copyright © 2009 by Frank Beddor. *The Looking Glass Wars*® is a trademark of
Automatic Pictures, Inc. Used by permission of Dial Books for Young Readers,
A Division of Penguin Young Readers Group, A Member of Penguin Group
(USA) Inc., 345 Hudson Street, New York, NY 10014. All rights reserved.

From *Princess Alyss of Wonderland* by Frank Beddor, illustrated by Catia Chien
and Vance Kovacs, Copyright © 2007 by Frank Beddor. Used by permission
of Dial Books for Young Readers, A Division of Penguin Young Readers Group,
A Member of Penguin Group (USA) Inc., 345 Hudson Street, New York, NY
10014. All rights reserved

Printed in Korea

1

978-0-9818737-4-9

This is not the story of a Mad Hatter

Nature does not hurry, yet everything is accomplished. —LAO TZU

Thank You

Scholars, Antiquarians,
Reasoners, Logicians, Rationalists,
and Knights Errant

# Contents

The Quest

The Rest

## Who are we?

The Hatter M Institute for Paranormal Travel is a devout assemblage of radical historians, cartographers and geographic theorists pledged to uncovering and documenting through the medium of sequential art the full spectrum journey of Hatter Madigan as he traversed our world from 1859-1872 searching for Princess Alyss of Wonderland.

You have dared to cross the threshold and enter our realm.
Come…let us take you to drink from the well.

# Introduction

Greetings fellow searchers and welcome to *Hatter M: The Nature of Wonder, Volume 3*, detailing and mapping the ongoing adventures of Royal Bodyguard Hatter Madigan, expert bladesman, and ranking High Cut of the Wonderland Millinery.

Pssst! Would you like to know a secret? Of course you would! We at the Institute believe few things in life are more satisfying than discovering a hidden history, cracking a code or knowing the specific knock that will open the door to illumination. Ahhhh the shiver of seeing a dusty, crumbling file authoritatively stamped TOP SECRET only to boldly open it and expose the truth for all to see.  Imagine the volume you now hold in your hands is stamped TOP SECRET and that when you open it you find yourself travelling through 1865 America with Hatter Madigan in search of answers  and finding secrets.

What hush hush 19TH century 'X-Files' bureau invented the ray rifle and steampowered rollarskates? Which president's zeal for the unknown and passion for fine headwear launched the search for White Illumination? Where did the famous 1960's slogan 'Flower Power' originate and what in the world does it mean?  What is hidden behind the locked door in Death Valley, California?

Now close your eyes and make a wish. If you wished for a secret map to guide you to the very nature of wonder then you are in luck. The map lies within. See you on the other side!

*The Hatter M Institute for Paranormal Travel*

What makes the desert beautiful is that somewhere it hides a well. —Antoine de Saint-Exupery

"Every individual is an expression of the whole realm of nature, a unique action of the total universe." –Alan Watts

Prologue

Once a prison...

...now...

...truly...

...an ASYLUM from the darkness that pervades the world. We are creating Wonderland here on earth.

You were Alyss at the bloody coup on her birthday!

I get to be Alyss fleeing with Hatter to the Pool of Tears.

No! You get to be Princess Alyss once she is lost somewhere in our world and no one knows where she is or what she is doing.

That's INSANE!

Remember Martha...

...this is just make believe... You don't really KILL anyone...

...this time.

My death scene will have them in tears!

Go!!! Take Alyss far from here.

Why am I here? I broke my own navigational
directive and traveled east away from the Glow.
And now as I tour this capitol city of unfinished
monuments and muddy streets, fragments of my
own city fly to mind in a rush of crystalline
images and light.  Could our worlds be more
different? And yet, the potential for good and
evil surely exists in both.

"To the dull mind nature is leaden.

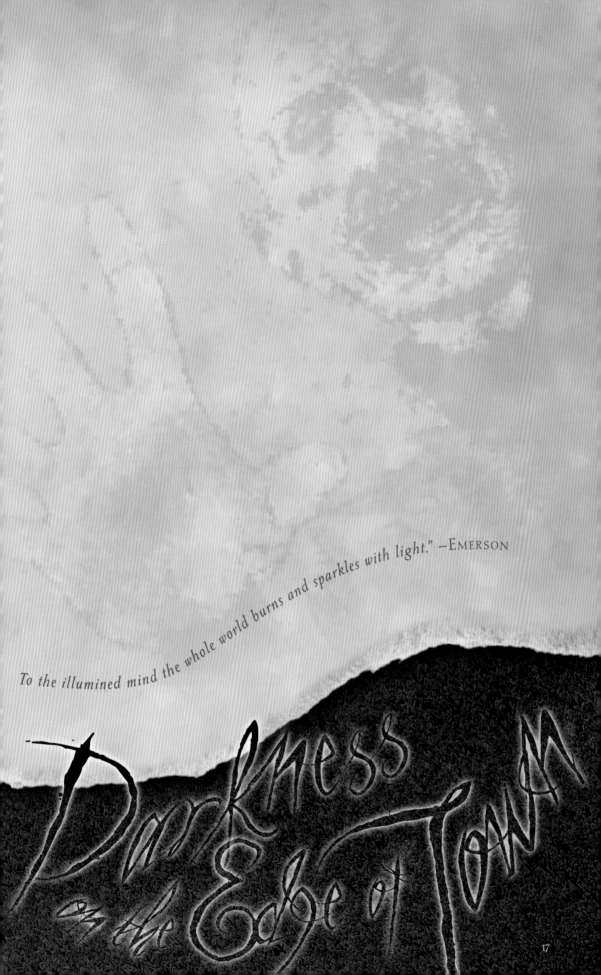

To the illumined mind the whole world burns and sparkles with light." —EMERSON

Darkness on the Edge of Town

20

BUREAU OF ILLUMINATED FORCES

Want a won ton?

A drop of distilled sunlight...

SSSSSS

BOOM

Lordy Lightning!

As I suspected... the dark luminescence. I must inform the President.

30

31

BUREAU OF
ILLUMINATED
FORCES

Hello, Philomena.

Horatio!

What did the President say?

It is imperative we are successful in discovering the antidote to this Black Plague.

Have you had any results?

I magnified a ray of sun and mixed it with a crystalline bath of dead sea salts. The molecular breakdown is highly energetic.

Let me see if I can find a chemical solvent to act as an active carrier.

In this capitol I have discovered much more than secrets, I have found illuminated minds willing to search for and exalt the light of Imagination. From my experience, I now believe that the brilliant equations of that mad mathematician who directed me here were a numerical manifestation of the Glow…leading me as always. Surely a power as vast as Imagination is not limited to one form.

Did Wonderland honor our Queen as they honored their President? Not with a forbidden procession or parade. But silently, yes.

*"The human spirit needs places where nature*

THE PHILADELPHIA PRESS

APRIL 15, 1865

Murder of Abraham Lincoln
President of the United States

has not been rearranged by the hand of man." —AUTHOR UNKNOWN

The Sound of Silence

49

51

Sorrow of

Our National
Calamity

# THE PHILADELPHIA PRESS

### APRIL 15, 1865

## Murder of Abraham Lincoln
## President of the United States

Treason culminated in
the Foulest of Crimes

A Skulking Assassin Fires
the Fatal Shot

THE FUNERAL CEREMONY
BEGAN AT THE WHITE HOUSE
ON THE 19TH OF APRIL
WHERE THE REMAINS OF
THE PRESIDENT LAY IN A
METALLIC COFFIN.

THE PROCESSION
STARTED FROM
THE WHITE HOUSE
AT 2 P.M. AND
PROCEEDED UP
PENNSYLVANIA
AVENUE TO THE
CAPITOL AMIDST
THE TOLLING OF
BELLS AND THE
FIRING OF
MINUTE-GUNS.

MOURNERS FOLLOWED
THE PROCESSION
TO THE CAPITOL. HERE THE
PROCESSION DISPERSED,
LEAVING THE REMAINS
OF THE PRESIDENT IN
THE ROTUNDA, WHERE
THEY WERE OPEN TO
VIEW THE NEXT DAY.

A spark, a shimmer, a radiance of luminescence explodes and suddenly I see past and present. I see a White Queen! And I see Imagination ruling a mindscape spanning both our worlds by the filament of Light. I must open my mind WIDE if I am to continue to be lead by such a force.

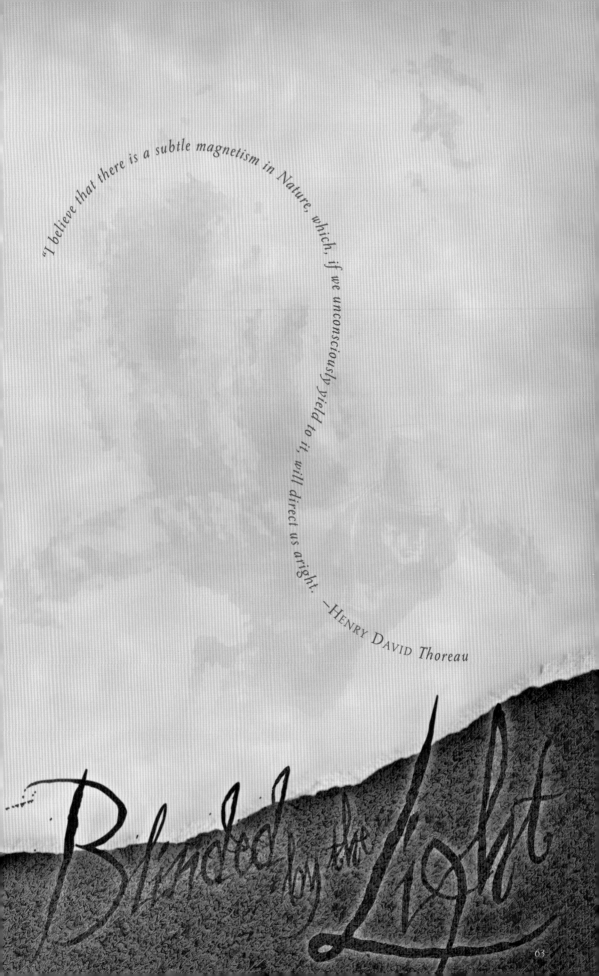

"I believe that there is a subtle magnetism in Nature, which, if we unconsciously yield to it, will direct us aright. —HENRY DAVID Thoreau

Blinded by the Light

73

WHAT IF DALTON CAN SAVE ONLY ONE PRINCESS?

HE'D HAVE TO SAVE PRINCESS ROSE BECAUSE SHE IS THE ELDEST.

WHO WILL SAVE PRINCESS GENEVIEVE?

I....

...WILL!

POPPER? HEARD YOU WERE IN THE PSYCHEZONE.

EARLY RELEASE FOR GOOD BEHAVIOR.

TWO AGAINST ONE!!

ONE HEART AGAINST TWO DIAMONDS? RUN WHILE YOU STILL CAN.

TELL THAT TO THE HATS.

FWIP FWAP

THRUM

FWOOSH

HOW'D THAT HAPPEN?

WHAT'S THE HAT TRICK?

DR-DROP ME.

SHUT UP.

HATTER?!

IS THAT POPPER'S REPLACEMENT?

YOU WORKING WITH HEART CADETS NOW? IS THIS YOUR BACK-UP? HA HA HA

HE'S QUITE ADORABLE. IF I WASN'T GOING TO KILL HIM I MIGHT KEEP HIM.

DROP YOUR WEAPONS, MADIGAN, AND I'LL DROP THE KID.

THIS ISN'T A NEGOTIATION.

HE ISN'T WITH ME.

AS FAR AS I'M CONCERNED YOU CAN TOSS HIM.

*We have located the caretakers of the source of White Luminescence but rather than appealing for their help, we must join with them in their battle against the dark forces intent on destruction. I have long contemplated that there was more meaning to my travels in this world than simply the return of Princess Alyss to Wonderland. While that is the primary motive of my quest, there is little doubt that the war waged in this world between White and Black Imagination is as powerful and critical as that waged in Wonderland. Is it the same war? Is it the same world?*

*My mission here is now clear. Every Queen needs a Bodyguard.*

Where

"Speak to the earth, and it shall teach thee." –JOB, 12:8

Have All the Flowers Gone

109

115

JOURNALS AND CORRESPONDENCE OF THE SOLDIERS PRESENT AT WHAT THE US CAVALRY LABELED THE 'WHITE FLOWER INCIDENT' ALMOST UNANIMOUSLY RECOUNT A MYSTICAL EXPERIENCE OF PEACE AND BEAUTY. WHILE MANY IMMEDIATELY RESIGNED THEIR MILITARY POST OR DESERTED TO RETURN HOME TO LOVED ONES, OTHERS REQUESTED NON-VIOLENT POSTINGS IN THE CAMP KITCHEN OR WORK AS MEDICS AND STRETCHER-BEARERS. MOST OF THE SOLDIERS WHO WITNESSED THE EVENTS AT THE WHITE FLOWER VILLAGE REFUSED TO EVER AGAIN SHOOT A GUN THAT FIRED LIVE AMMUNITION, WHILE THOSE THAT DID – WENT MAD.

WHERE DID HATTER MADIGAN WANDER IN SEARCH OF WONDER? IT APPEARS FROM THIS HAND DRAWN MAP DISCOVERED INSIDE HIS JOURNAL THAT REALM KEPT HER PROMISE TO GUIDE HATTER TO SECRET LOCATIONS IN OUR WORLD WHERE THE ENERGY OF WONDERLAND COULD BE ACCESSED. ALAS, THE LOST PRINCESS WAS NOT WAITING FOR HATTER IN ANY OF THESE LOCATIONS BUT EVIDENTLY SOMETHING OF GREAT VALUE WAS. WHY ELSE WOULD HE HAVE DRAWN THE MAP?

Aerial majesty illuminates the moment... I am beginning to see the light. (2)

The wind has stopped and the petals are still as Smith unlocks the secret door to wonder. (8)

An image of predictability giving way to pure randomness. I surrender to the winds of change and follow the petals. (1)

PACIFIC

OCEAN

Is it this world's pool of tears? A puddle where no puddle should be? Should I enter this Portal? But no... the petals blow north! (7)

MEXICO

The propulsive power of nature's imagination... astounds and energizes me. (3)

Beneath the surface lies the mystery of the caves. Vast imaginative power locked inside crystal... hidden inside this world. Waiting. (4)

I hear the harmonic chord as it echoes into eternity. A call to collaborate with my unconscious? (5)

It is the time of the caterpillar breaking apart... being destroyed... so that the butterflies will appear and fly. (6)

**WHERE WAS HE?**

1 - ARIZONA (GRAND CANYON)
2 - JUNEAU, ALASKA (NORTHERN LIGHTS)
3 - YELLOWSTONE PARK, WYOMING (OLD FAITHFUL)
4 - DUBUQUE, IOWA (CRYSTAL LAKE CAVES)
5 - MORRISON, COLORADO (RED ROCKS AMPHITHEATER)
6 - ANGANGEO, MEXICO (MONARCH BUTTERFLY MIGRATION)
7 - SAN DIEGO, CALIFORNIA (PAVED OVER PORTAL TO WONDERLAND?)
8 - DEATH VALLEY, CALIFORNIA (ONE OF THE LOST GHOST TOWNS)

While it is true that every Queen needs a Bodyguard for protection, it is also true that every Bodyguard needs a Queen to lead. Realm shared the wonders of her world and they have brought me here to a reunion of sorts. Lost in space and time, lead only by the petals of White Luminescence, I allowed myself to wander and trust that the Glow would manifest in unforeseen ways to guide me.

Finding life in a place called Death, I open myself to further discoveries.

*"A rose is a rose is a rose."* —Gertrude Stein

Back Garden
to the G

WHAT COSMIC COMPASS HAS LED ME ACROSS HEMISPHERE AND TERRAIN?

THE SACRED GEOMETRY OF ANGLE, SPIRAL AND PHI?

THE FLOWER OF LIFE?

LOVE?

?

THERE ARE ONLY EVER TWO REASONS TO CROSS AN OCEAN: LOVE AND DUTY.

EVEN FEWER TO CROSS A DESERT.

WHICH OF THE TWO DROVE ME WEST ACROSS THE AMERICAS IN SEARCH OF MY WARD?

WAS IT LOVE?

OR DUTY?

OR ARE THEY NOW, FOR ME, THE SAME?

ONE HAT. ONE HATTER. TO CONTAIN AND CONTROL.

TO SERVE AND SUSTAIN.

MY HAT TATTERED...

MY BLADES BROKEN...

...MY BOOTS WORN PAPER THIN...

IN THE DEAD PLACES I JOURNEY BY NIGHT SURE-FOOTED AND UNDER COVER THIRSTY BARGAINING WITH MY GUT AND GULLET...

BUT SOMEWHERE IN THE DISTANCE, A LIGHT...

THERE IS AN UNWRITTEN LINE OF THE CODE NOW, I AM ITS AUTHOR "IN UTTER DESPAIR, YOUR FINEST HAT IS HOPE."

THE BREEZE IS WARM YET KIND THE STARS ARE AGLOW BUT NOT WITH THE GLOW I SEEK...

A PURPLE SKY, A WATCHFUL MOON, BUT NONE AS IMPORTANT AS THIS MY DESTINATION.

AND IN THAT VALLEY IS A TOWN, AN OLD WESTERN TOWN AND IT GLOWS

A TWILIGHT OF A DIFFERENT SORT

129

131

The city of San Francisco... through a puddle where—

No puddle should be!

So VERY glad to meet you Smith Dobson.

And your name, sir?

Hatter Madigan—

Of the illustrious Madigan family?!

Both my parents and my brother were Milliners.

And I made blades for all of them. I remember young Dalton— I sewed his first coat.

And you would have sewed mine but I was still at the Academy.

What has brought a Millinery Man this far from Wonderland?

Like yourself...

...the pool claimed another victim...

But I should say... VICTIMS. I was traveling with my charge.

Who?

THE WHISPERING WOODS

IS THE QUEEN DEAD?

DALTON! WHAT HAPPENED?!

IS IT TRUE? IS SHE... DEAD?

I KNOW. GOODBYE, BROTHER.

I HAVE FAILED MY CHARGE.

I AM DISGRACED. THERE IS NO PLACE IN WONDERLAND FOR ME.

BUT DALTON...

...NO ONE EVER COMES BACK!

THE LOST MILLINER'S ARMORY WORKSHOP

As you see... I have been waiting for you.

You have been waiting for me?

Not you in particular.

It was a SENSE I had that I should prepare in the event a Millinery Man should ever require my service.

Smith... in my time here I have visited 422 hat shops in over 100 countries because of a SENSE I had that someday, somewhere I would find assistance in my search.

Well, then. Remove your coat and let me get to work.

137

144

145

If only the nature of man was one of wonder. Such a world this would be!

*"In nature there are neither rewards nor punishments;*

there are consequences." –Robert Green Ingersoll

Epilogue

151

# HATTER M
## THE ZEN OF WONDER

### VOLUME FOUR

WELCOME!
East meets West!
Japan's first ambassadors to San Francisco arrived today via two sailing ships, the Kanrin Maru and the USS Powhatan. Enthusiastic crowds lined the docks to greet and cheer the Japanese delegation of artists, leaders and most notably, samurai warriors!

することはできませんこのいまいましいボートを降りて待って！*

彼らは良いがサキ...*

サキのものがたくさん！*

*Translated from Japanese:
"Can't wait to get off this damn boat!"
"They better have saki..."
"LOTS of saki!"

Here they come! Get ready with those cannons!

HURRAH!

Cannon go BOOM!

WELCOME TO SAN FRANCISCO!

As the ships docked and the gangplanks were lowered a welcoming 21 gun salute was fired to hail San Francisco's far east visitors.

The exotic samurais in their traditional robes known as ki-mo-nos and hemp sandals drew appreciative "oohs" and "gollys" as well as some unfortunate taunts from the gathered throng.

Oooooh!

Golly!

In A-mer-i-ca men wear britches!

Go back to your tiny island in that there skirt!

These highly trained Japanese warriors have come to San Francisco in peace to honor the open trade agreement that will make both our nations strong and RICH!

Each samurai displayed a sheathed sword at their waist. These priceless swords are both ceremonial and martial and highly valued by the Japanese culture. A samurai without his sword in battle is like a cowboy without his horse in the desert... as good as dead.

# Illuminated

## WASHINGTON D.C.
### Where All the Secrets are Kept

The turmoil of the final days of the Civil War and the assassination of President Abraham Lincoln left Washington shrouded in secrecy. Nearly 150 years later our own inquisitive Colonel Barlow arrived in Washington to investigate the entries revealed in Hatter's journal for publication in this volume. In the course of his forensic research on Hatter's travels he uncovered many scintillating details, one of which still lies buried in our nation's capitol….

What was hidden inside the unfinished Washington monument?

Construction commenced in 1848, but by 1858, the government was out of money, leaving the Washington Monument to sit unfinished until 1878 when work resumed.

### Ambitious Actor or Agent of Black Imagination?

Theorists here at the Hatter Institute have pondered the connection between Wonderland's Dark Watchers, the reflective bound agents for Redd and the gunman who assassinated President Lincoln. Could the Dark Watchers have influenced John Wilkes Boothe in his decision to kill the president? Was there a Wonderland connection? Yes and No. Evidence gathered regarding other participants in the Lincoln plot indicates that the original intent of the conspirators had been to kidnap the President. In this planned kidnapping we see the dark hand of the Watchers as their mission was to kidnap and drain Lincoln's imagination. Boothe's maniacal need for attention and a dramatic ending (actors!) evidently upset everyone's plans…including Redd's.

### Deposed General Early…where did he run to?

After Dr. Obsidian Stoker hijacked his command by distributing vials of Black Imagination, General Jubal Early was spotted stealing a pair of bib overalls off a Virginia clothesline. When the Army of Northern Virginia surrendered on April 9, 1865, Early, disguised as a farmer, fled to Mexico.

### What's Lincoln hiding under his hat?

In the midst of this swampy frontier capitol of wooden wheels and outhouses there was an exceptionally forward agency of avant futurists. This was Lincoln's top secret society for paranormal investigations that he named… *The Illuminated Forces.*

*Forces*

## The Bureau of Illuminated Forces
### Who were Lincoln's enlightened investigators?

ILLUMINATED FORCES
Agent's Identity Card
Name. Horatio Alabaster
Signature. *Horatio Alabaster*
By Special Order of
President Abraham Lincoln

Horatio Alabaster was Lincoln's trusted confidante. Together they shared an expanded awareness of what they termed, THE BIG IF. Lincoln authorized the establishment of the Bureau of Illuminated Forces as a top secret investigative agency for the study of paranormal and metaphysical mysteries.

ILLUMINATED FORCES
Agent's Identity Card
Name. Philomena Ark
Signature. *Philomena Ark*
By Special Order of
President Abraham Lincoln

Alabaster recruited the teenage Philomena Ark after her expulsion from the Betsy Ross finishing school for burning a flag when her unauthorized experiment with sun lasers went awry.

When Royal Bodyguard Hatter Madigan traveled to Washington D.C. in April 1865, he initially discovered the raw, unfinished capitol of a young nation in the final days of a civil war. But within hours of his arrival, the telltale Glow of Imagination led Hatter to the very center of this enigmatic paradigm of power.

The Bureau of Illuminated Forces was indeed secret. Colonel Barlow had to dig deep to uncover these images and records. But the biggest secret of all was yet to be discovered! Shall we explore further? Turn the page…

Futuristic conveyances were a passion of Alabaster and his development of vehicles for land, sea and sky rivaled Jules Verne for their audacity and ingenuity. Here is one of his early steam powered carriages.

← A PROPELLER AT THE BACK?

← HORSES

KEROSINE LAMPS AT THE SIDES

SOME KIND OF MOTORLIKE THING BETWEEN THE FRONT WHEELS?

Steam powered rollerskates were Philomena and Alabaster's preferred mode of navigating the crowded streets of Washington D.C.

W e followed Hatter and the Illuminated Forces west in search of the White Flower Tribe using a model of the compass first invented by Horatio Alabaster. The essence of this compass is its ability to direct the bearer towards the highest energy at the same time as providing geographic direction. Genius!

**The Alabaster Compass — a marvel of energy and geography.**

Armed with the 'Alabaster Compass' the Institutes' resident raconteur Miss Emily McGuiness went on a fact finding mission that lead her deep into the hidden history of the White Flower Tribe to answer the question: Where DID all the flowers go?

## Report from the Grand Canyon

From Hatter's journal we knew that the White Flower Tribe fled their sacred lands rather than be moved to a reservation. As Chief Petal explained his tribe's ancient directive, "Should our enemies become too vast for the White Flowers to remain on the surface of this world we must go underground." UNDERGROUND? Little remains in our modern world that has not already been explored, bought and sold except that which is 'OFF LIMITS' to the public. And this is where the trail began…with a secret!

According to an article appearing in the Phoenix Gazette on April 5, 1909 the explorer G.E. Kincaid made an astounding discovery deep within the Grand Canyon of an enormous underground citadel. Briefly recounted, here is his story:

"First, I would impress that the cavern is nearly inaccessible. The entrance is 1,486 feet down the sheer canyon wall. It is located on government land and no visitor will be allowed there under penalty of trespass. The story of how I found the cavern has been related, but in a paragraph: I was journeying down the Colorado River in a boat, alone, looking for minerals. Some forty two miles up the river from the El Tovar Crystal canyon, I saw on the east wall, stains in the sedimentary formation about 2,000 feet above the river bed. There was no trail to this point, but I finally reached it with great difficulty. Above a shelf, which hid it from view from the river, was the mouth of the cave. There are steps leading from this entrance some thirty yards to what was, at the time the cavern was inhabited, the level of the river. When I saw the chisel marks on the wall inside the entrance, I became interested, securing my gun and went in."

# Flower Tribe

Following the navigational directives of the *Phoenix Gazette* article Miss Emily – minus gun – entered the cave described by Mr. Kincaid.

As she trekked nearly a mile underground, the long main passage lead to another mammoth chamber from which radiated scores of passageways. Several hundred rooms were discovered, reached by passageways running from the main passage, one of them having been explored are 854 feet and another 634 feet.

This message written on the wall of the cave in petalglyphics first alerted her to the hidden underground village of the White Flower Tribe.

Translated from the White Flower language:
BEWARE NEW AMERICANS!
Someday…YOU will be the Indians….

## Flower Power

The spoken language of the White Flower Indians had been recorded by Hatter (an inter-realm linguist par excellence) in his journal. Working from this guide, Miss Emily was able to enlighten herself with the White Flower lexicon prior to entering the caves. The White Flower language is unique in that it is composed of the names of white flowers from around the world that are then inscribed in the flowery petalglyphics that convey written communication. Other samples of petal graffiti found included "Flower Power!" and the story of "The Cloud that Exploded into Flames" which recounts the saga of the Illuminated Airship crashing to the ground and Hatter Madigan coming to assist Realm in restoring her Imaginative Powers.

To read more on the secret caves: www.homehighlight.org/entertainment-and-recreation/nature/the-grand-canyon-s-grand-secret.html

# Stacking the Deck

Since our discovery of the first lost card linking the Wonderland cards discovered by Frank Beddor in the British Museum and the deck collected by British antiquities dealer Mr. Buffington with Hatter Madigan, royal bodyguard and artist, we have continued stacking the deck for our mutual edification. The card drawn by Hatter Madigan while incarcerated at the Lunatic Asylum for the Mad and Disillusioned depicting Wonderland's Millinery H.A.T.B.O.X. was what initially tipped us to this invaluable source material. For some unknown reason that card remained at the asylum while the others in the deck had disappeared. This naturally whetted our investigative appetite and we spent the last year circling the globe following possible leads as to where the other cards in the deck may have been... shuffled. Behold before you the most recent color art images inspired by Hatter Madigan's cards and rendered by our very own Institute artists.

# Princess Alyss

Alyss on her mother's throne.

Now, after nearly 150 years, the cards can be reunited in their original box.

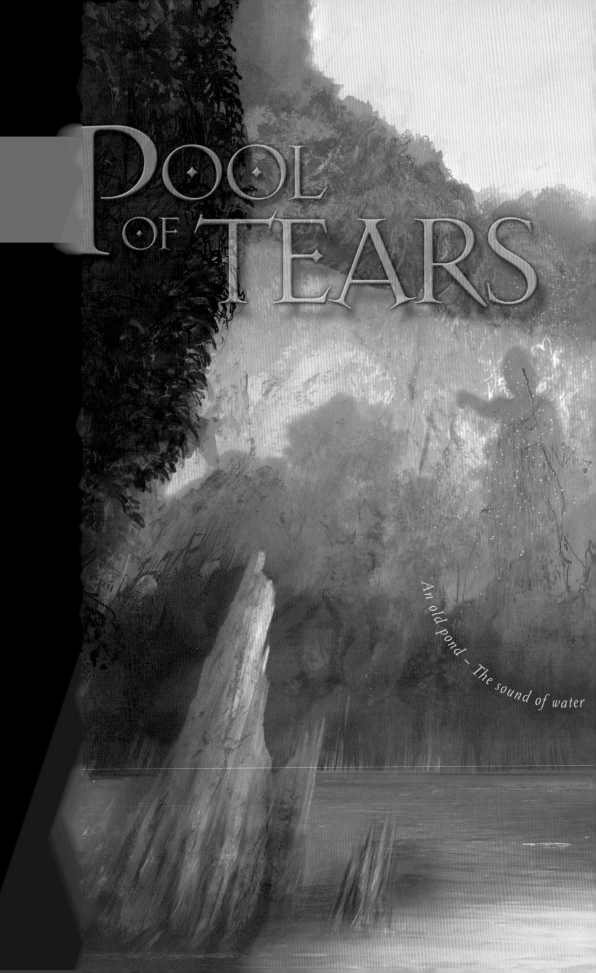

# POOL OF TEARS

*An old pond – The sound of water*

When a frog jumps in. —BASHO

*Nature is an infinite sphere whose center is everywhere*

# HEART PALACE

# Bibwit Harte

*and whose circumference is nowhere.* —Blaise Pascal

All things are artificial,

# THE MILLINERY

# HOUSE OF CARDS

*for nature is the art of God.* —THOMAS BROWNE

GENERAL
DOPPEL

*Nature, to be commanded, must be obeyed.* —Francis Bacon

# GÄNGER

# Alyss in Exile

## Friday before Tea

When mother ordered Hatter to take me and leave Wonderland, we fled through a looking glass that took us to the Whispering Woods. Once in the woods Hatter held me tight and ran faster than a spirit-dane. At last we came to the cliff above the Pool of Tears. It is said that no one ever comes back from the Pool of Tears, but Hatter assured me I would because I would one day return to be Queen. And then we jumped, but not soon enough, as The Cat's long claws raked out across my birthday gown and tore away a piece. He nearly got me!

But before I could scream we hit the water . . .

The Pool of Tears shimmered like a liquid looking glass.

An excellent record of Alyss' determination to return to Wonderland via a "puddle where no puddle should be" is seen in the annotated map of London. I find this cartographic treasure simultaneously heartbreaking and hopeful, as it details the lost princess' search for the puddle that would take her home.

## Friday after tea

. . . I know Hatter held me as tight as he could but a tremendous force tore us apart. Poor Hatter! He had promised my mother to keep me safe and Hatters always keep their promises, especially royal bodyguards. I tried to smile to let him know I would be okay, but the water smooshed my face in all different directions and I shot down very, very fast and then I shot up even faster and found myself in this world called London.

Alone.

## Sunday morning

My arrival in this world called London was sudden and frightening. I shot up and out of the puddle and found myself standing in the middle of a crowded avenue. Everything was spinning and I was cold and lost and AFRAID. Where was my mother? And where was my royal bodyguard? In desperation I began to jump in puddle after puddle searching for the way home. Then I saw a boy watching me and he was smiling and I knew I wasn't alone anymore. I was about to meet the most honorable

### Quigley Gaffer

I vow to discover the secret of puddle travel! There simply must be a way of knowing which puddle is THE PUDDLE!

"I found a puddle right in the middle of Hyde Park. It didn't work!"

· MAP OF LONDON ·

Discovering and testing puddles kept me very busy since it seemed to rain every day!

I am CERTAIN that this puddle must still exist and it is up to ME to find it.

Splish!

Splashh!

Sploosh!

As many of our readers know, following the publication of the Looking Glass Wars, we were contacted by the British historian Dame Agnes MacKenzie. Her startling missive informed us that a trunk had been discovered in Oxford, England containing the art and journals of a young Victorian girl. Of course, the contents of this trunk had once belonged to Princess Alyss Heart of Wonderland. Since Alyss and her ordeal are at the very center of Hatter's quest we believe the insights gained from her art and journals provide valuable juxtaposition for all serious Hatter scholars. →

## Sunday . . . raining

Quigley brought me to an alley where he and a group of other very ragged, thin children lived. Everyone was curious as to who I was and where I had come from, so I told them about Wonderland.

They all loved my stories but unfortunately, they couldn't eat them. What could I do to help? As I was thinking I noticed a sad little flower in a cracked pot lying in the alley. To amuse my new friends I began to imagine the flower humming and then singing in a beautiful high-pitched voice. Quigley and the others were amazed. That's when I knew what to do!

## Sunday . . . still raining

We became street performers. I would imagine the flower singing and Quigley would gather the coins tossed by those who stopped to listen. Our first show was a hit. The next show even bigger. Each day we made enough coins to feed everyone very, VERY well.

As thoughtful readers of Dickens will recall, orphans, urchins and estranged children were an all too common sight on the sooty streets of nineteenth-century London. It seems from Alyss' journal that she was accepted into a den of street urchins by the boy named Quigley. While Quigley was an open-hearted generous sort, the others insisted Princess Alyss pull her own weight in foraging for food and rags. Alyss' solution was, of course, to use her imagination.

The boy in this photo reminds me of my friend Quigley.

They believed I was a REAL PRINCESS.

Who was this lost princess living among the uninformed and non-curious citizens of Oxford?

Once again we *creak* open Alyss's trunk to give you a look inside the heart and mind of Wonderland's most imaginative exile.

LA LA LA LA OOOOH LA LA LA LAAAAAAA!

Sunday . . . more rain

And then something extraordinarily horrible happened. My imagination began to weaken. Each day the flower's voice grew fainter and fainter until it stopped singing. I could not explain to myself let alone the others how I had failed. My imagination had always been with me. To have it fade was like losing my last connection to Wonderland. To eat, we all had to go back to stealing food from the markets. One day we were caught by a pack of London bobbies. The other kids escaped but I was nabbed and taken to the most frightening place I had ever seen, The Charing Cross Orphanage.

I never saw Quigley again, though I still look for him.

I had named the flower 'Tralaaa.' She truly loved to sing and I will always remember the last few notes of her last song...

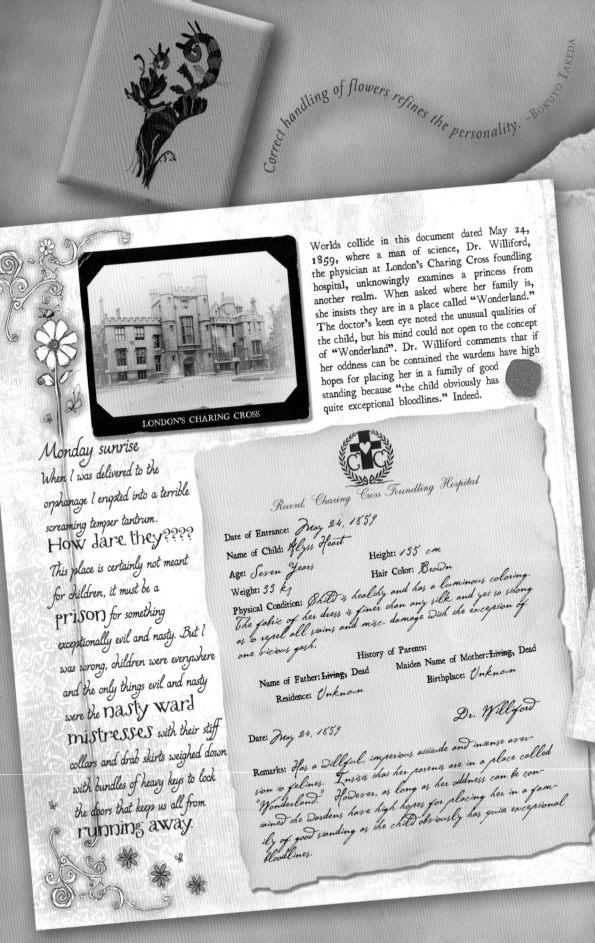

Worlds collide in this document dated May 24, 1859, where a man of science, Dr. Williford, the physician at London's Charing Cross foundling hospital, unknowingly examines a princess from another realm. When asked where her family is, she insists they are in a place called "Wonderland." The doctor's keen eye noted the unusual qualities of the child, but his mind could not open to the concept of "Wonderland". Dr. Williford comments that if her oddness can be contained the wardens have high hopes for placing her in a family of good standing because "the child obviously has quite exceptional bloodlines." Indeed.

LONDON'S CHARING CROSS

## Monday sunrise

When I was delivered to the orphanage I erupted into a terrible screaming temper tantrum.

### How dare they????

This place is certainly not meant for children, it must be a **prison** for something exceptionally evil and nasty. But I was wrong, children were everywhere and the only things evil and nasty were the **nasty ward mistresses** with their stiff collars and drab skirts weighed down with bundles of heavy keys to lock the doors that keep us all from **running away.**

*Record, Charing Cross Foundling Hospital*

Date of Entrance: *May 24, 1859*

Name of Child: *Alyss Heart*     Height: *135 cm*

Age: *Seven Years*     Hair Color: *Brown*

Weight: *33 kg*

Physical Condition: *Child is healthy and has a luminous coloring. The fabric of her dress is finer than any silk and yet so strong as to repel all stains and misc. damage with the exception of one vicious gash.*

History of Parents:

Name of Father: ~~Living~~, Dead     Maiden Name of Mother: ~~Living~~, Dead

Residence: *Unknown*     Birthplace: *Unknown*

*Dr. Williford*

Date: *May 24, 1859*

Remarks: *Has a willful, imperious attitude and intense aversion to felines. Insists that her parents are in a place called "Wonderland." However, as long as her oddness can be contained the wardens have high hopes for placing her in a family of good standing as the child obviously has quite exceptional bloodlines.*

## Tuesday

I look forward to **escaping into my dreams** each night, but even this has become unbearable because my dreams now have a very **unwelcome visitor . . .**

## THE CAT!

One night I decided that rather than being **frightened** of what was chasing me, I would imagine that I was running toward something **BEAUTIFUL**.

There were endless doors lining the halls and I imagined I would find my mother if I opened the **very last door.**

But when the door opened, instead of seeing her I saw all her favorite **flowers.**

And I could smell her favorite perfume. It smells very **PINK** and **I love it.**

Each night it sneaks into my sleep and invades my dreams with its growlss hisses and hot, stinky cat breath!

Dreams are only night-mares if you let them do what they wish.

RETURN TO SENDER

Queen Genevieve
On the other side
of the looking glass
WONDERLAND

Look deep into nature, and then you will understand everything better. —ALBERT EINSTEIN

## Wednesday

I was adopted by a very dull and unimaginative family named Liddell and brought to live in their home in Christ Church, Oxford. Living in a home was very different from living in a palace, and I found it difficult to adjust, as I believe ANY princess would.

'Alice' and her sisters Edith and Lorina at Christchurch, photographed by Charles Dodgeson

I hoped the rain had come from Wonderland so the PUDDLES would take me HOME.

Everything was so small and smelled rather of burned vegetables, while my bedchamber was just ridiculous. THE BED DIDN'T EVEN FLOAT! How could I even begin to get a perfect night's sleep???? The Liddells refuse to believe in Wonderland or that a real princess could come to their world and even though I repeatedly corrected them, they insisted on changing my name to Alice.

### HOW RUDE!!!!!

Uncertain of their adopted daughter's bloodlines and wishing to make a suitable marriage (a prince perhaps???), the Liddells chose to keep her origin top secret by destroying all records of the adoption, even going so far as to forge an "Alice Liddell" birth certificate, which modern genealogical forensics easily exposed to be false! The child was simply not born in this world.

| 1 | 2 | 3 | 4 | 5 | 6 | 7 | 8 | 9 | 10 |
|---|---|---|---|---|---|---|---|---|---|
| Name, if any | Sex | Name and surname of father | Name, surname and maiden surname of mother | Occupation of father | Signature, description and residence of informant | | | When registered | Signature of registrar |
| Alice | girl | Henry Liddell | Lorina Hann Reeve | Dean of Westminster School | Humphry Ward, Westminster, London, England | | | 1852 | Humphry Ward |

REGISTRATION DISTRICT: Westminster

....Birth in the Sub-district of....Westminster....in the County of London

Hope and fear cannot alter the seasons. –CHOGYAM TRUNGPA

My
unimaginative
Oxford family.

Mr and Mrs. Liddell
(equally gloomy
on all occasions)

Cruel
Governess Pricks
(she actually prefers
sour to sweet!)

Proper sister
Lorina
(a grown-up lady
in the body of a
little girl)

AND ME.
If it weren't
for my
hollizalea
headdress
and mini
rainbow cloud
I should fear
becoming just
like them!

Baby Edith
(there may still be
hope for her)

Thursday
full moon!
In Wonderland I always
remembered my dreams. Why am I unable to remember my dreams now . . . ? Aha!
I was not sleeping in a dreamgown! When I inquired of Mrs. Liddell when I would be fitted
for my dreamgown she looked alarmed. I explained that in Wonderland
there were special gowns in which you slept to capture your dreams. I had closets full of dreamgowns in
Wonderland but requested only ONE for here. I thought I was being quite modest, but Mrs. Liddell
opened her mouth very wide and shouted at me, "You must STOP
your incessant impossible imagining. Really now,
I think you dream too much as it is, ALICE!" Dream Too Much???
How sad to think that anyone could ever dream TOO MUCH.
I spent the rest of the day locked in my dark little dungeon
of a bedroom, imagining and drawing dreamgowns . . .

The dreams would be reflected on the gown
the next morning so you wouldn't forget
ANYTHING important.

My
favorite.
I ALWAYS
dream in
color.

The human spirit needs places where nature has not been rearranged by the hand of man. —Author Unknown

WONDERLAND
by Myss Heot

180

Everdear Mother,

I have been looking for you in every looking glass but I cannot find you! Please knock or call out loudly if you see me passing by the looking glass you are behind, because I am afraid I will never find you and I am so lonely for you. I miss you but I am trying to be brave and strong and remember all the ways a princess must behave to be a good queen.

I love love LOVE LOVE LOVE LOVE you you you YOU

Alyss

*Turn the page for a special preview of*

# ARCHENEMY

*Book Three in the* Looking Glass Wars® *trilogy.*

# PROLOGUE

Oxford, England. 1875.

Alyss of Wonderland raced up the front walk, using her imagination to unlock the door and turn the latch. Inside the house, nothing had changed. The umbrella stand and hat rack, the family pictures hanging in the hall, even the gouge in the baseboard marking where she'd thrown her ice skates one winter afternoon: Everything was exactly as it had been when she'd lived there . . . so long ago, it seemed.

"Please, what do you want?" the dean's voice reached her from the back of the house.

She sighted them in her imagination's eye: the dean and Mrs. Liddell, Edith and Lorina. Their clothes a good deal ripped, they huddled together on the drawing room sofa in fearful silence while

Ripkins—one of King Arch's bodyguards, and a deadly assassin—stood ominously before them. Ripkins: the only Boarderlander who could flex his fingertips, pushing deadly sawteeth up out of the skin in the pattern of his fingerprints.

"Please," the dean said again.

Fingerprint blades flexed, Ripkins moved his hands fast in front of him, shredding air. Mrs. Liddell flinched. The assassin took a step toward the dean, the sisters each let out a sob and—

"Hello?" Alyss called, walking directly into the room. She had imagined herself into Alice Liddell's long skirt and blouse, her hair in a tight bun. "Excuse me, I didn't know there was company."

She tried to look startled—eyes wide, mouth half open, head tilted apologetically—as she thought her double would. Wanting to catch Ripkins off guard, she pretended to be meek, cowed, and let him grab her and push her toward the Liddells.

Where he'd touched her, there was blood.

Ripkins' hands became a blur in front of him, churning air and moving in toward the dean's chest. Alyss had no choice but to expose her imaginative powers in front of the Liddells. With the slightest of movements, she conjured a deck of razor-cards and sent them cutting through the air.

Fiss! Fiss, fiss, fiss!

In a single swift motion, Ripkins spun clear and unholstered a crystal shooter, firing a retaliatory cannonade. Alyss gestured as if wiping condensation off a looking glass and the shrapnel-like bullets of wulfenite and barite crystal clattered to the floor.

The Liddells sat dumbfounded, their fear muted in the shock of seeing their adopted daughter engage in combat, producing otherworldly missiles out of the air—flat blade-edged rectangles resembling playing cards, bursts of gleaming bullets. She conjured them as fast as she defended herself against them, what with the intruder making expert use of the strange guns and knives strapped to his belt, thighs, biceps, and forearms.

"Father!"

A fistful of mind riders—ordinary-looking darts infused with poison that turned victims one upon the other in rage—rocketed toward the family.

Alyss threw out her hand and the weapons changed trajectory, shooting toward her. She annihilated them in midair with a pinch of her fingers, becoming like gravity itself, pulling whatever Ripkins hurled at the Liddells toward her until—

The wall pushed out a score of daggers. Ripkins, knocked backward by a steel playing card as big as a man, slammed against them and slumped to the floor.

Silence, except for the ticking of a grandfather clock.

"Oh!"

In the doorway stood Alyss' double, the woman she had, with utmost effort, imagined into being to take her place in this world: Alice Liddell who, with her gentleman friend, Reginald Hargreaves, stared at the dead assassin and Wonderland's queen. The dean, his wife, and his daughters looked from Alyss Heart to Alice Liddell and back again.

"I—?" the dean started.

But that was all he managed before Alyss bolted from the room and out of the house, sprinting until she was well along St. Aldate's Street. Certain the Liddells weren't following her, she walked briskly in the direction of Carfax Tower, toward the portal that would return her to Wonderland: a puddle where no puddle should be, in the middle of sun-drenched pavement behind the tower. But even from this distance she could see that something wasn't right. The portal was shrinking, its edges drying up fast. She started to run, her imagination's eye scanning the town.

"How can it be?" she breathed, because all of the portals were shrinking, the tower puddle already half its former size when she leapt for it, closing her eyes and sucking in her breath, anticipating the swift watery descent through portal waters, the reverse pull of the Pool of Tears, the—

Knees jarring, she landed on pavement. The portal had evaporated.

Alyss Heart, the rightful queen of Wonderland, was stranded on Earth.